DREAMS IN A
NIGHTMARE

Senjuti Mazumder

Chennai • Bangalore

CLEVER FOX PUBLISHING
Chennai, India

Published by CLEVER FOX PUBLISHING 2022
Copyright © Senjuti Mazumder 2022

All Rights Reserved.
ISBN: 978-93-93229-49-6

This book has been published with all reasonable efforts taken to make the material error-free after the consent of the author. No part of this book shall be used, reproduced in any manner whatsoever without written permission from the author, except in the case of brief quotations embodied in critical articles and reviews.

The Author of this book is solely responsible and liable for its content including but not limited to the views, representations, descriptions, statements, information, opinions and references ["Content"]. The Content of this book shall not constitute or be construed or deemed to reflect the opinion or expression of the Publisher or Editor. Neither the Publisher nor Editor endorse or approve the Content of this book or guarantee the reliability, accuracy or completeness of the Content published herein and do not make any representations or warranties of any kind, express or implied, including but not limited to the implied warranties of merchantability, fitness for a particular purpose. The Publisher and Editor shall not be liable whatsoever for any errors, omissions, whether such errors or omissions result from negligence, accident, or any other cause or claims for loss or damages of any kind, including without limitation, indirect or consequential loss or damage arising out of use, inability to use, or about the reliability, accuracy or sufficiency of the information contained in this book.

To my mom and dad,

who never gave up on me

INTRODUCTION

Poetry helps us relate to the world. It is through the words of poetry that a poet is able to express their inner feelings.

I have always read books and to be particular I started reading poetry as it helped me relieve my feelings. I discovered many poets during this journey and it is amazing how the poems reflected my thoughts and feelings.

The beauty of poetry is that you can feel what the poet is trying to express by playing with words and also realize how one is not alone in the journey of life.

It is through poetry that I understood that there are people who feel the same as me and suddenly I did not feel that alone anymore.

I would love to quote one of my all time favourite Emily Dickinson- "If I read a book and it makes my whole body so cold no fire can ever warm me, I know that is poetry." I started writing this collection with no

INTRODUCTION

thought in my head; I was just staring at my ceiling and that is when I began this journey.

This collection of poetry is where I have expressed my thoughts and it is from several experiences some of it are my own and some from my imagination but most of the poems are dedicated to the people around me.

I hope whoever reads this book can feel my words flow in them, as the words take them on a magical journey.

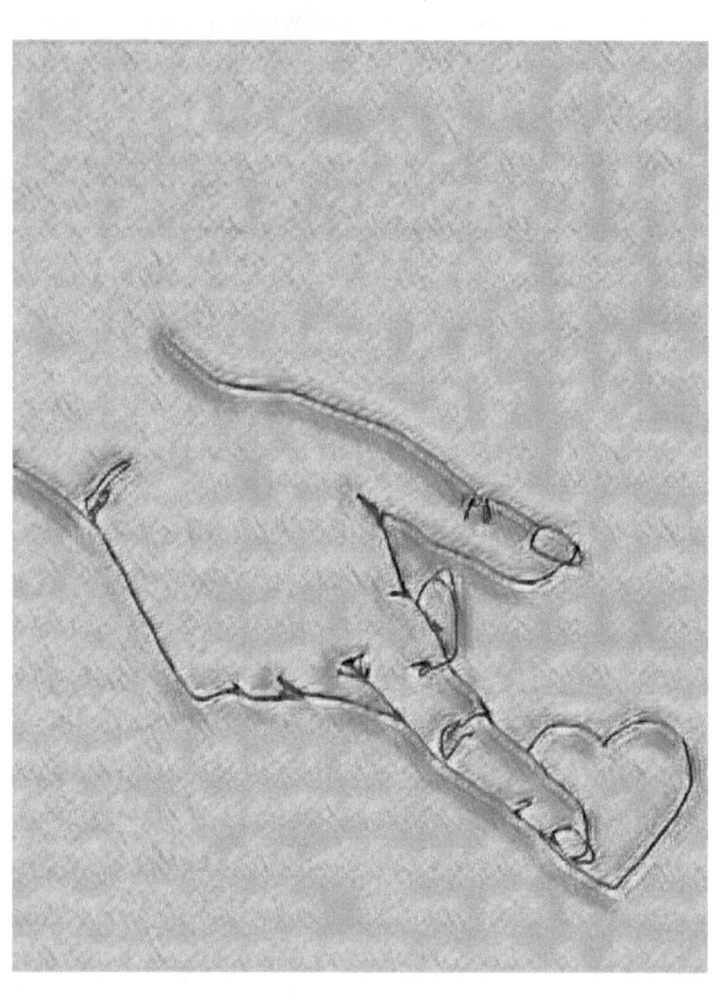

POEM 1

Our tale is like a misunderstanding that drives a gap
Into a corner
I don't understand what is wrong with us
Because it is still blinking
For your promise
The feeling of missing is still bitter
We slowly familiarise with each other

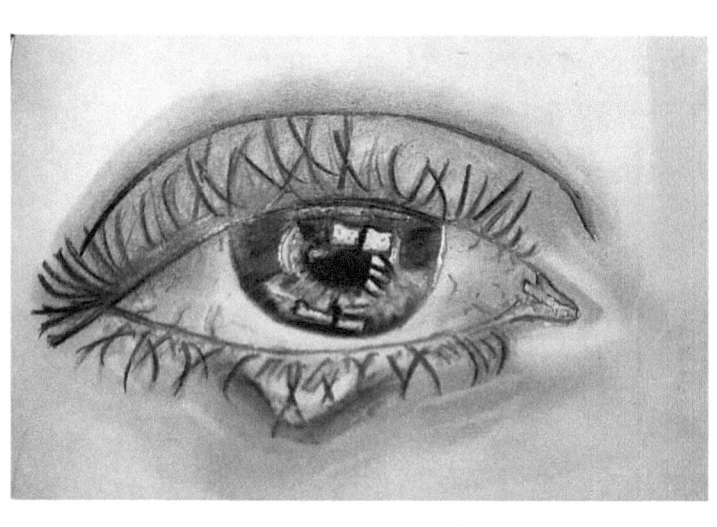

POEM 2

I looked at my phone
Stared at the screen
And my ears ringed with the song
Notifications kept popping up
None of them were yours

I have ignored people for weeks now
This whole thing feels unreal
I can't believe I fell so hard
My heart never aches in this kind of love
Because I always knew you weren't real

Not real for me
Cause you don't know me
You will never know me
This love is just mine and
Will always be mine

POEM 3

I heard you sing
The sea breeze hitting you
Your deep voice made my heart flutter
I looked into your deep black eyes
And you stared at me with your boxy smile

You pointed at the sea like a child
Exploring the world
You seemed excited about everything
I saw the spark in your eyes
Started humming the song on my own

I heard my mom call me
Suddenly pulling me back to the reality
I stared at you for the last time
Realising you never saw me
A faint smiled formed on my lips
And then I got back to my books.

POEM 4

He sat there alone
His eyes were a perfect spring sky,
His mind clear and his smile warmer than the gentle sun.
In those blue eyes were the sweetest threads of caramel.

Seeing him after three long years
I realised I had never actually 'dealt with it'
I was taken back to the past
Where I have wove dreams of our love
The woven dreams were like the end of a rainbow.

"How are you?"
His deep husky voice had the same effect on me;
I looked at him and almost stammered
He thought that I overreacted;
But little did he know how much I loved him.

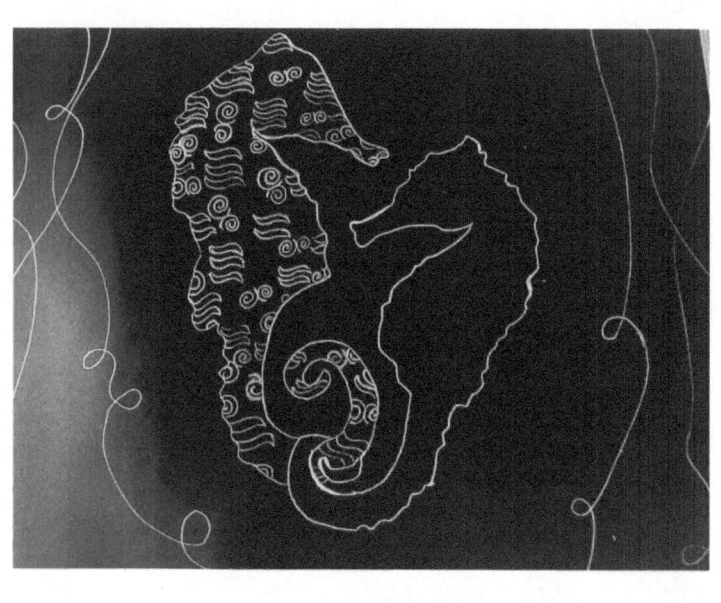

POEM 5

Wandering lonely in the vastness
Ocean is a mighty harmonist
It's been long
A millennium!
People stare but no one cares
Faces pressed against the glass
Trapped in a prison
Being constantly watched
Hidden conceptual mechanics
Rising through depths of minds
The sea horses whispered
And cried being stuck
In an aquarium.

POEM 6

It was the ninth of November
We met in the church
The first time I saw you smile
Shivers ran down my spine
Do you remember the day we had our first kiss?
The day you stood under the lamp-post
Wished you never have to see me again
It all happened in the month of November

It is the ninth of November
The sky seems clear
I stare at the stars and try to find you
You disappeared into sky last November
No time left for me to kiss you goodbye
The flames rose into the sky
Tears down my cheeks
I waited for you darling
Only to find the lamp-post by my side
The month of November is like a dream to you
A nightmare to me.

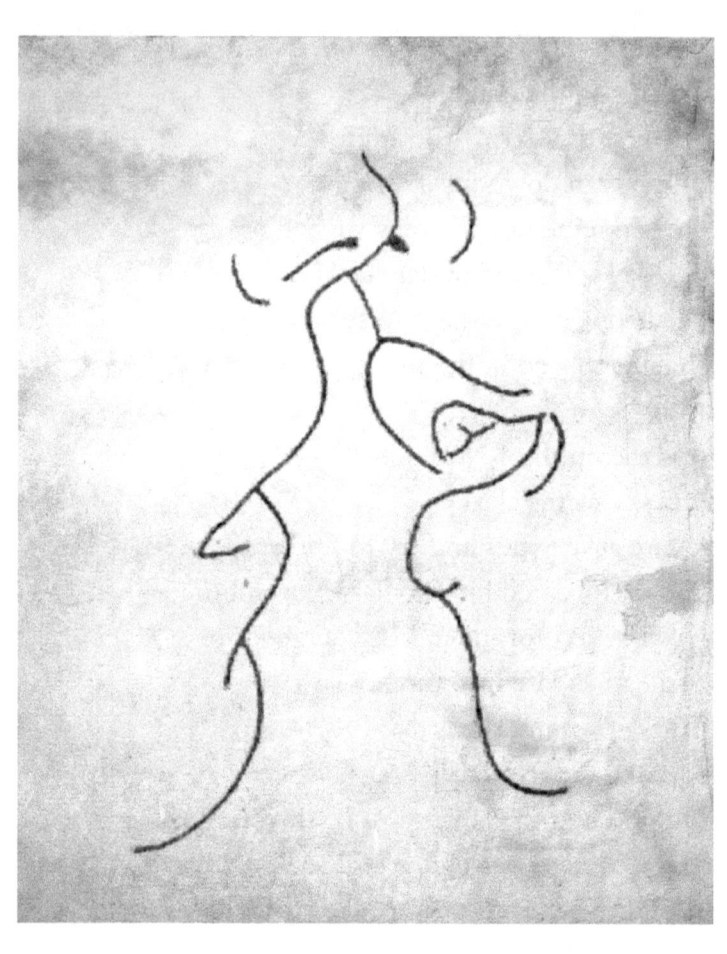

POEM 7

We got out of the class
Called my dad and stood there
My intuition telling me something's on
I stared nervously at my screen
I was scared and excited for a reason unknown
I played our favourite song "Perfect"
I could hear your low hum
I hummed it along with you
You stood outside the gate
In all black and a smile that made me jittery
The street light flickered dimly
My friend stood behind me
Busy with her phone
My cheeks turned crimson as I almost stepped out
with butterflies in my stomach
I seem small beside you
You bent down as your hands trailed down my cheeks
I shivered at your touch
Unknowingly my eyes shut
As soon as your lips touched mine
I pushed you
I don't remember your lips touching mine
I can't recall the moment not even a second of it

I heard my dad's car and ran away from there
Without sparing another glance
I felt the whole world spinning around me
Jumped inside the car and couldn't hide my smile
I felt like I was burning as I turned up the volume and rolled down the car window
Plugged in my earphones and kept smiling
The cool September wind hit my face
I calmed my nerves realising
You will leave me
Came in terms with the truth
"Stop lying to yourself"
Tears rolled down my eyes
I wiped my face
Took a deep breath and put on a smile
I smiled through the pain
That is the end of our almost first kiss

POEM 8

These days I am so sick of crying
I seem to stay locked in my room
Left alone with my thoughts
Wondering if it was all my fault

I can always smell your woodsy scent;
I can hear your deep voice,
It calls me when I -
Am walking in a dark alley

With the countless stars guiding me with their twinkling light,
I see you standing there at the end of the alley
At last I reach for your hand
Only to see you fading away.

POEM 9

Full of hate, shame and gloom.
Lying in my bed, I stare at my ceiling.
Wondering why we couldn't be together.
Uncontrollable tears stream down my face.
I curl myself into a ball trying to control myself.

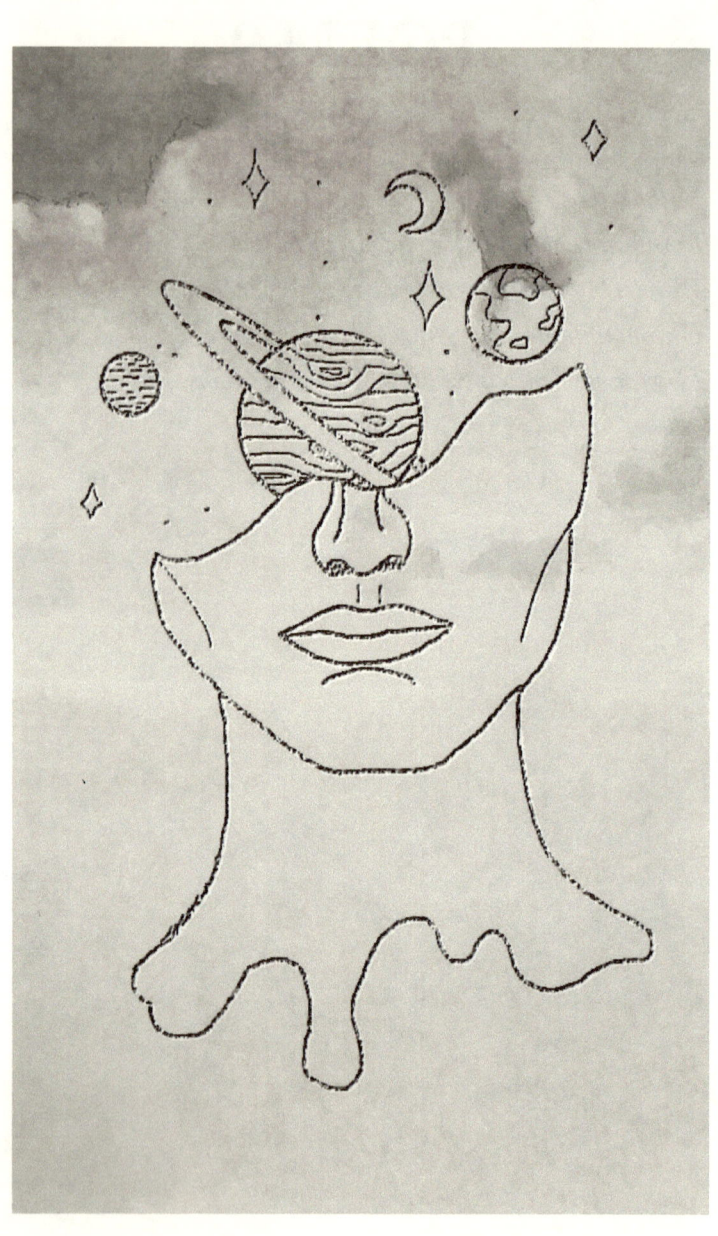

POEM 10

The stars twinkled in the sky at midnight
Your face was shining brightly in the moonlight
I can't forget your touch
Your smile and your deep whisper
'I love you' these three words made my heart flutter with joy
But who knew those words meant nothing to you
I soon curled up into a ball
Whimpering from the pain of rejection.

POEM 11

You showed me dreams
That I never imagined of
You promised me fragment of life
I took it to be true
The cold wind made my hair flow
I smiled
Pretended like nothing happened
Continued to be friends
Always stood there
When you wanted to vent out
Your anger, frustration on someone
My pillow soaked in cold tears
Yet I kept smiling
Pretended it was all okay

POEM II

POEM 12

I sit in silence,
Pale and cold, tears frozen
Steady thrum of heartbeats
I am afraid to let go.

POEM 13

I decided to start holding your hand and travel the world
Raise our heads to catch the star and the sky and make a wish
Love maybe a lesson in life
I may be the one destined for you in this life
When I was young I read a fairly tale book in my mind I always had a wish
One day I want to be like Cinderella together with the price riding a white horse
I desperately look for it
Why I can't find it? I turned around only to find you to stay by my side and never leave that is why you are my true love.

POEM 14

Feeling a little bit lonely tonight,
My coffee lost its warmest comfort
Crying can't fix it, tears on my face
The uncertain feeling makes me exhausted
This vague relationship has misunderstanding and distance
Can the one in my mind fill the hole in my heart I know we don't match you are missing the one in your heart.
I need your company but I dare not say I feel aggrieved and embarrassed
I may not be special to you but I only have feelings for you back to back comfort being quite in love and being omitted slowly.
Being worried that a short sunny day will be blue anytime
Love makes me optimistic being able to stand around you is a sweet favour.
I know we don't match you are missing the one in your heart.
I need your company but I dare not say
I feel aggrieved and embarrassed
I may not be special to you
But I only have feelings for you back to back comfort
Being quite in love and being omitted slowly.

POEM 15

I believed the last night was the last time I saw you
Your face was the hope for my empty soul
You blamed me for everything that happened
But the pain I feel in my heart is too much to bear

I believed that you were running away from me
Suddenly realizing you were never here
The moments I believed we had were
All just part of your plan

I still choose to believe in the past
We spent together making memories
I thought we were in love
But I never knew it was always me alone

I will still be the one
Saying sorry, taking the blame on me
My friends always ask me why I apologise
I stare blankly at them not knowing what to say

I don't regret loving you
But I also wish it would somehow be different

I still can sense the warmth of your hands
I still smile thinking about the silly jokes

I remember you bringing my favourite ice cream
I stared at you as warmth spread across my face
The ice cream melting down the cone dirtying my hands
You laughed looking at my clumsiness

I miss you but not because
I loved you but because you were never mine
I had you for a moment but I didn't
I will always wait for you in our secret place.

POEM 16

I ran through fire for you ;
Now my love for you is ashes.
You act as if I owed you love,
But you give me only apathy.

I miss you not in a deep aching way but
In the low hum of my mom's car radio,
I sit with my guitar
Playing D minor on repeat.

As I drift into dreamland.
Where we are in love
Dancing to our favourite song:

As you slowly lie down on the lavender field,
Pulling me beside you
Wrapping your arms around my waist;
I smell like you.

The woodsy smell covered my being
As you suddenly stand up
Running into the darkness
The end which I never expected.

I lay there in the backseat
Of the car dreaming
Of us being together
But it never ends with a forever.

POEM 17

Our world was in danger
Under purple skies you came to me
And lead me into the light
The ocean ride

But never broken in two
I felt you all around

And my heart beats under the same ocean
The ocean that hates me
The ocean that calls my name
Give it a chance fight for your love

When will your fingers touch the ocean?
When will the day shine in your heart?
Dance in a storm
Waves can swing wide

I believed I was sinking like a stone
I was like an ocean you were a river

And my heart beats under the same ocean
The ocean that hates me
The ocean that calls my name
Give it a chance fight for your love

POEM 18

She laid there motionless
Death had taken her in the chariot
Decorated with beautiful dark roses
Only he understood her
Told her she will soon find peace
Took her to the world
Welcomed her with smiling faces
No one pushed her aside
Had her own little family there
Never spoke about the past
She found love for the first time
Death brought her love

POEM 19

I look up at the stars
The star that shines in the darkness
I am welcomed by the constellations
And the pale crescent moon.

I want to float away into
This vastness joining the constellations
And dance with the angels
In an everlasting dream
I want to be free.

POEM 20

They found me on the way to school
Frozen to death they said
No one knew I froze myself
To run away with death
To have a peace within me
Yes I am selfish as they said
I won't let them hurt me anymore
I am free
Free like a bird

POEM 21

Death they said scared them
I loved it, he passed by us everyday
He stared at me and smiled
Told me I am loved
Never questioned my thoughts
I am selfish they said
But they made me like this
I can't feel emotions like before
I can't love like before
Can't hold hands, can't hug or kiss
Death had taken me with him
I left with a smile; a tear froze on my rosy cheeks

POEM 22

She looked up wanting to speak
Stared at the darkness,
The moon disappeared as if to support others
She knows no one can love her
She is hated by all
"Love" she did not know what it was
The cold wind blew and slapped against her face
She still promised herself
To fulfil her parents' wishes
So that they can keep their heads high

POEM 23

You always say you love me,
But do you really know me,
I saw you from somewhere in the back rows
Cheering and waving at you
Hoping for you to notice me

Your wide eyes
And strong hands, and soft touch,
Speak to me in hushed tones
I stand there staring at you

As for me, my heart goes wild
With mad love and adoration for you,
So much that when I try to speak
The words stumble and I am tongue tied

There are butterflies running wild in my body
I always try to figure out what is going on?
I never realised love can be this strong
It is scary to fall in love

So it always ends with you and me
And the quiet

And the way we both lack a way with words,
Yet the comfortable silence we share
Amplifies the light of love
Bursting in our hearts.

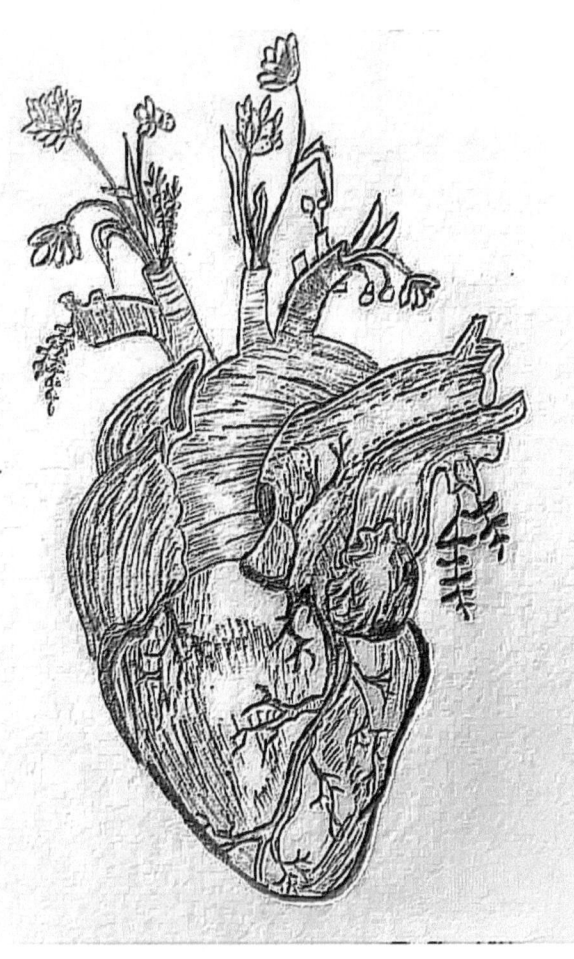

POEM 24

I am but a wilted flower
I am only a dream.
Your memory is my only companion
As I clasp my hands and cry
I get down on my knees
The sadness burns

They say, all good things must end.

POEM 25

Am I too naive?
I freeze in front of you
When you turn around
Even time stops
I can only hear my heartbeat.

POEM 26

We had a love so pure;
But our passion was just a broken dream
And forever meant only a flash,
I would have followed you through a dream
But our love was just a wish unfilled;
Our kiss was a figment of pledge
I would have waited for you always;
true love you promised
But we are now just two lonely souls.

POEM 27

Returning back to school
After the session break
Waited for a bus with hope
Thought this year will be better
Hope is the only thing we can keep
Faith in and let go of our pessimistic thoughts
Saw the same yellow bus
Students in green
Talking and smiling like buds blooming
In spring, their faces had tints of red and pink
Making them look more beautiful
I made my way beside the window
Looked outside as the bus took off
The wind hit my face and I finally smiled
Humming "Love story" finally
Letting my emotions flow
I reached the same old place
Which has been a home
For nine years

POEM 28

I sat by the window as
The sweet smell of spring
Filled my being
From the flowers that hid from view
I stared at the blue sky
Winter had laid down her icy bouquet

After a tiring day at school
I was waiting for the bus to start
One by one people stepped in
They were effusive and
Their faces had turned crimson From all the races they had

Someone came up to me and sat beside me
I smiled at this little bud
Who had sparks in her eyes
And hope to bloom
Bloom into a beautiful flower
Her big doe eyes spoke a lot of things

I could sense it so I smiled again
This time to myself
For finding this bud who
Wanted to explore the world
For she was a precious flower
On her way to bloom

I felt the need to protect her
Childlike innocence
She is a little bud who
Thinks the world to be as beautiful as her

POEM 29

It has been a few days
Since the first day after session break
I am my usual self
Letting my soul absorb the calming wind
That hit my face

I saw the little bud again
As the bus started off
I began humming with my eyes shut
I felt a pair of orb staring at me
I turned opening my eyes
Saw the most beautiful black twilight eyes.

Her black eyes seemed to me
The poetry of the universe,
Told in moments,
Moments that weave together
That form the fabric of our lives.

POEM 30

'Rose' the name craved in my heart forever
Travelling on that same old bus for ten years
Never had I met someone as beautiful
As the little bud
She held onto my hand pulling me beside her
She had something in her
That attracted me
Kept me alive and somehow she always had things to talk about
It used to be random and still the pair of twilight orbs
Shone as the moon made its way up to the sky
In winters we saw the sun hiding behind the mountains
As the bus took us to our destiny.

POEM 31

Soon it was time for me to change schools
Two years went by in the blink of an eye
The last day, I remember her pulling me beside her and
She sang 'Stay a Little Longer with Me'
Her voice was like a bird that was free
Spreading its wings as it rose higher up in the sky.

POEM 32

She was the little bud that I wished in my life
We went on long drives after school
The car radio was like a low hum
I heard her voice as she told me about her say
I smiled looking at her
Her voice was nothing but a sweet melody to my ears
We drove the beach
It was 5 p.m. "Why are we here" she asked
She had hope in her eyes
I smiled as I pointed at the setting sun
The sky painted blood orange
We hummed 'Love Story'
As our voices wove together to form a tapestry
Of the heart visible to the souls present.

POEM 33

I used to get lost in her eyes
Those dreamy black
She made me think believe in angels once again
I was like a baby exploring the world
She made me believe in love once again
I loved how she asked me
"Are you okay?"
I always nodded as an answer
Somehow she knew I was not
And she filled me with her warmth
I miss her interruptions
Those hugs and the way she giggled when I glared at her
All I do is get lost in our memories.

POEM 34

She came into my life
Lit it up with all the bright lights
She had scars too
Scars that only I knew about
She was full of goodness
People asked me what made her stand out
She believed people will change
She believed everyone deserved second chances
She forgave everyone
She was cheated a thousand times but never gave up
All because she believed that everyone had a bad journey.

POEM 35

All I want to say to the little bud
Now all grown up
In the city that I once lived in
The city that holds all my dark past
She is there in lighting up the world
With her warmth and brightness
Thank you little one for helping me see the world
With the eyes of love.
For making me believe that love can win.

POEM 36

I am driven back to the day
You said you have found someone better
The colour in my face faded
We stood under the mistletoe
I still wanted to taste your strawberry lips

For the last time I wanted to feel your hug
It was Christmas Eve
Lovers were cuddling under cosy blankets
Wishing for happy endings

I stood there like a lifeless doll,
As you words kept ringing in my head
People pushed me at the entrance
As they rushed in and out of the restuarant

The air around smelled like roasted turkey
The only thing I could smell was
My heart burning
There was mirth and laughter all around
I could hear my heart shatter into million pieces
As it hit the ground

You left me standing there
Under the mistletoe as you walked away
Love grows under a mistletoe
And you ending our love under a mistletoe

POEM 37

I remember your arms wrapped around me
And I let my head rest upon your chest.
All my thoughts stopped
As if my heart took over
My head when we were close.

I was always scared
Scared of losing you
Losing the love we had
Here I am today on the same spot
The winter evening looks like how it was two years ago
I saw you again today

You looked happy
She is pretty and maybe better than me
In many ways, things I would hate to imagine
I saw it in front of me

Her blonde hair drooped around her pale cheeks
Her glossy locks lifted by the wind
Her pink lips slightly parted
As I saw you look at her
With love as pull her closer to you

Tears came as if,
At long last,
my accumulated ocean of brine
Was trickling through.

POEM 38

The air is filled with
Smell of freshly baked cookies
The streets were as busy as popcorn on a skillet
Life used to be like a bowl of cherries
Now it seems to be empty and dull

You left me with promises
Just like a pie in the sky
Your smell faded away from my clothes
Just like you faded away into the darkness

Christmas is coming around
I see happy faces
And couples holding hands
Smiling and leaning on each other
Keeping each other warm
Just like you and me
They walk down the path filled with joy

POEM 39

As Christmas approaches
I miss you and the smell of hot chocolate
You made for me
And I hear the bells jingle outside
Laughter of the children
And people bargaining
In the shops at the side of the street

The dim street light
Flickering on and off
Like the day
You held my hands and kept them warm
I was lost in your eyes
As you bent over to kiss my lips
You smelled like the mixture of lavender and rose

We walked back home
The house smelled like vanilla
Your hands around my waist
You left wet kisses on my neck
As I leaned back on your chest
And took in the smell of your floral colongue

The fuzzy winter pyjamas
You left for me before
You left me behind like the melting snow
I waited for you
But soon winter
Laid down her icy bouquet
And now it is Christmas again

Another Christmas without you
I stare into the darkness
Hoping to see your smile
A smile that was like a sudden beam of sunlight
Illuminating the darkest corners of the room.

POEM 40

Christmas is near
And I am thinking of us
Our memories of being together
Under the mistletoe.

That is how we met
When the sky was black
And the earth was white
I walked in my winter boots
As the snow crackled under my foot

I walked as the snow fell
On my Amber hair
We met each other
At the entrance
Of the Lover's Bar

We were lost in each other's eyes
Yours deep as the ocean
While mine dark as the midnight
We were pulled back to earth
As we heard people say
"Kiss! Kiss!"

We failed to notice the mistletoe
Under which we stood
That is what we call love at first sight
Or should we call it love under the mistletoe.

POEM 41

When I called and said it's over
I didn't mean to give a free pass.
A free pass to call me and text me
Whenever you are bored.

I left you because we were not right;
I always tried to keep up but
Love can't be built with one's effort,
It needs to be mutual babe.

The free pass was for you leave
But you do it everytime!
Using me whenever you are bored
Breaking me time and time again.

POEM 42

Take a bow
I am but a broken dream
your breath burns the body
forever in your stare
your pictures washed away by time

POEM 43

Everytime I feel like
I have moved on
Leaving behind the bits and pieces of past
I start smiling for the first time in years
Not a fake smile anymore
Can you not disrupt my peace?

I was feeling a bit better
And then suddenly
Came in a notification
"Ting" the sound still ringing in my head

My hands were frozen
Cheeks crimson red
Shivering I picked up my phone
You manage to mess things up with one single message

You did that again today
Once again when I thought I was done
You made me feel like a shit
My friends told me you are a jerk

I never ever said a bad thing about you

Yet you make me feel like it was all my fault
You make me suffer everyday
Every minute I regret my choice

Mistakes are made
And we learn a new lesson from those
But what you taught me
Was Love doesn't exist
And trusting someone is the biggest mistake we can make.

POEM 44

They stared at each other
Piercing their souls
As millions of stars stared at them
Their breath hitched
Their throats went dry

Soon they couldn't breathe
They couldn't move an inch
The fire came as a golden ball
Igniting the night
As it outshone the stars.

POEM 45

I am not good at expressing.
But I can feel your emotions
I can make you feel the joy of life
I can make promises
And never break them.

I am the type who believes in
Fate and Destiny
I am the flame and the spark,
Risen from the ashes
I see the ray of light
A new beginning!

The world outside seems cruel
But have you ever sat in your room;
Trying to notice how lonely they are
Have you thought about them who are
Lying on the road holding on to their lives?

I have, I have seen smiles
On a tear stained face
I have seen happy faces silently
Begging to let them free.

POEM 46

I found you in my dreams.
Beside the disc of brightest blue;
The lake is the finest of mirrors,
Brighter than our dreams.

The aurora lights played above as the woven threads of our souls.
His eyes were a marriage of light browns and sage greens,
And what I saw was the ambient hue.
His eyes is the place my soul finds nirvana.

I have been marked with all of life's crayons,
You look into my eyes and see nothing
But a murky shade of turquoise and cyan.
You were so close to me that I could smell the after shave;

Let's kiss like it is our last
Bidding farewell to each other, you pushed your ruffled hair
Making me giggle for the last time.
All I can see is dark realising the spell of love was broken.

POEM 47

She looked at the room for the last time
The room where she had built her dreams
She never loved saying goodbyes
She decided to run away
Far away from all the worries
Of the world
Found him standing there
His ocean blue eyes shining
In the moonlit night
Their souls held hands
They smiled at each other
Their journey ended with
Their love frozen in their souls

POEM 48

Told you many times
I feel like dancing in the midnight
Looking at the moon
Among millions of stars
Staring at the sky
Holding your hand i want to sway
Around like a princess
Who was trapped in the castle
Laughing and dancing with you
Under millions of star

POEM 49

In you I see the chance
For the kind of love they say doesn't exist anymore.
The love that makes us feel ecstatic,
The type that lasts even when our souls leave us

I want a love that's passion,
And a love that lasts,
A love that will turn up into flames
And calm the ocean waves.

Yet is also a serenity of souls
That can dwell in forever.
It's not the kind of love everyone can deal with;
So come if you dare.

It takes courage to walk
Into the light after a lifetime of shadows;
It takes the heart of a fighter, a survivor;
To love someone so deep

A love that is so warm,
That can make the coldness of a heart disappear
So darling, love me if you dare
Forever or a second, let's give love a chance.

POEM 50

Loving you made me realise
How it feels like to be burnt
Loving you is like letting you play with my heart
Snowflakes touch my hand
As I fall on my knees
On the white land underneath
Breathing heavily as I let you pull the trigger
Letting the bullet hit me
Forcing me onto the ground
Smiling I let my soul free
From the pain it suffered.

POEM 51

Found a guy in the dark
He held my hand tight
Always tried to save me from
The dark and the unknown

Waited for me in the cold
Dressed in red I walked down the stairs
He held me close by my waist
As he smiled at me

I miss the days
Being young and reckless
All I want is to be loved
And loved like I never felt the pain.

POEM 52

Smelling like the Hawaii beaches
You came to me
I looked at you wondering what have you been upto?
Then i saw that boxy smile of yours

I knew you were upto something
A mischievous smile but
The most beautiful smile i ever saw
I loved how it was only for me

I loved how only i got those warm hugs
And those kisses
I loved how you interrupt me with sudden kisses
Kisses that smelled like strawberries.

Everyday I see you enter my dreamland
And leave when I wake up
But I relax when I see you
Sleeping like a kid.

All curled up beside me
Your arms wrapped around my waist
Pulling me in as I giggle
I see you smile and my heart calms down.

POEM 53

I still remember how you held me
On the cold December night

The snowflakes on my curly brown hair
I looked at you with a hidden hope
I saw faith in your eyes
Eyes that looked only with love

Your arms around me tight
Pulling me in, letting me a smell
The beauty of your heart
I fell in love with you in the first sight.

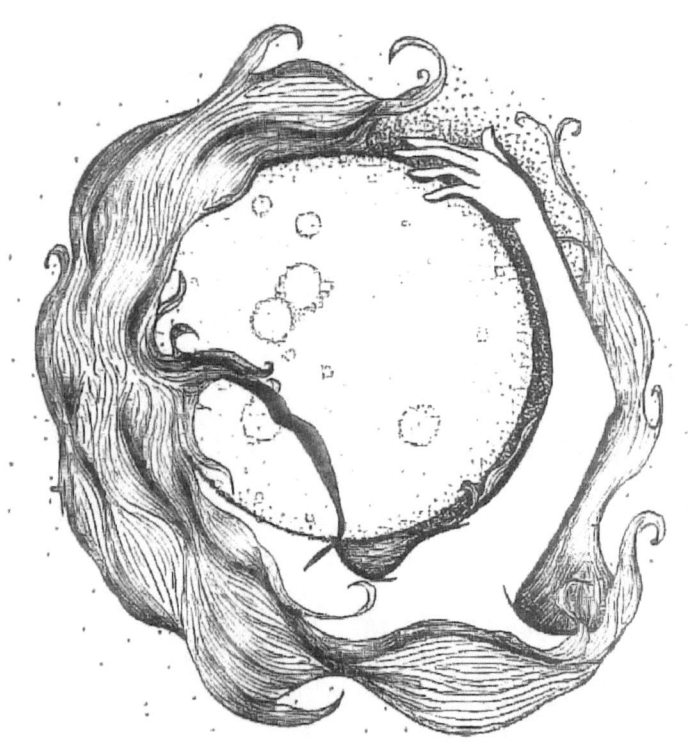

POEM 54

Never seen you face to face babe
But somehow I still love you
A small smile on your face can make my day good
And when you cry, I can't stop
The tears roll down my cheeks

I am just an ordinary girl
Living in a small city
One of the millions
Who chase you all day.

I look at you and wonder if you are okay?
Everyday I wait for your message
But soon I feel lonely and
I drown myself under
Deep in the ocean of my dream.

POEM 55

In those days, so tired of crying
I want to thank you
Letting me breathe
You held me tight in your arms
Showing me how beautiful love can be

I did the things wrong
If I fall in love again
I promise to do it right this time
Not for me but for you love.

POEM 56

If my love for you is true and deep
You know that I can let go off you too
Loving you doesn't stop me from letting you go
All you did was blame me for leaving you

Have you ever wondered what it felt like to me
I was the one in love
You just played with that love
I don't blame you, I allowed you to take control

All you say is let's end the past
Do you think I don't want to?
I want to forget it,
I want to believe it never happened

But you blame me, you
You blame my friend for supporting me
I, what am I to you dear?
Just a rebound right?

A thing you can use whenever you need
Throw away when not needed
And again get it back within seconds
I hate it because i let you have this kind of power over me.

POEM 57

Love!
Love is a word that makes
Us feel happy, peaceful and it feels like
We are flying in the sky
Free and spreading our wings and hugging the blue
sky

Love makes us feel peace
It makes us happy
But what if love breaks you
What if love kills you

Can you save your heart
From suffering the pain
Of heartbreak or rather betrayal?
Can you breathe and smile like
You did?

Do you remember the glow you had on your face?
Do you remember how you smiled?
He made you feel weak
You gave your all

He played with it like
His toy cars and he remembers
About you when he is bored
Just like the basket full of
His childhood memories
Kept carefully somewhere.

Love is the word i am scared of the most
He still scares me
The thought of falling in love
Is like giving someone
The power to destroy me piece by piece.

POEM 58

I hope you see this
A letter to my lover
We were together for the last few years
You made me feel butterflies
All over my body

And once I let those fly
You made me feel bad
Bad about myself,
Leading me to the beach
You pushed me deep into the ocean.

The ocean, is the world
Full of magic
You allowed me to escape the cruel world
My love, thank you
For letting me see

See the magic that
Lies beyond the world
I love you darling for
Showing me how cruel the world can be
And for guiding me towards peace

POEM 59

The sky was dark and gloomy
All the colours in the sun
It turned grey
I wait for the seven colours to splatter in the sky.

The rainbow draws itself upon this blessed sky;
Painting the sky like its own canvas,
Bringing out the colours
That spark a wonder that stays within.

It is like God's graffiti,
Drawn with perfection in the dreary sky.
I saw the twin rainbow, double arches painted into the
Silver- velvet above.

I watch and allow
My spirit to fly
As the colours slowly fade
Into the bold sky.

POEM 60

He leans forwards,
His warm breath in my ear,
He then hums the song we used to dance to in high-school
My lips, the ones that really didn't want to smile tonight,
Creep into a grin.

He keeps on humming
Until I take him in a bear hug
And kiss him.
I swear he is an expert on keeping my heart beating,
Without him I'm sure it would simply stop.

We lay naked in the moonlight,
Waves crashing the shore not far away,
His arms wrapped around my waist
He lent in for a kiss,
The kind I wanted to last forever,
But after a time he withdrew to
Gaze at my burning crimson face.

"Do you know I love you?"

He asked as his hand pushed my hair from my face
My lips broke into a grin as I shook my head
And managed to say "No"

"Well I do and you know what?"
I shifted my gaze and stared into
His big doe eyes
"I always will"
His gaze had intensity
His love was like a kerosene and
I seemed to be its only flame.

POEM 61

Feelings of love,
Can bring you ecstatic feelings
At the same time can take you to
Ride a rollercoaster of emotions.

POEM 62

Memories I will never be able to go back to,
They fly through the screen of my mind,
Every moment turn as fast flipping pages
Everything used to be simple
And I could breathe without an anchor pulling me down,
The world was beautiful
It was like a dream, a far away dream
I can still feel the wind
Slapping against my face;
I loved how I ran barefoot on the lively grass;
My laughter echoing through the bright yellow fields.
I always wonder if I can go back to those days
Where innocence played the most important role
Now the world seems to tie me down with its burdens
The pain and agony of longing to go back as I begin to let go
The memories in my mind suddenly disappear.

Bringing me back to the present,
Lying on my back, staring into darkness.

POEM 63

I see him standing
Amidst the purple ocean
Full of joy like a vivid rainbow,
I watch him show his boxy smile.

I ran to him
The flowers in the field sway
In the wind, and the air is filled
With a fruity smell.

I am standing there in a nice
Red dress, staring as the sky
Speaks in thousand colours
Splashed in red, pink and orange.

The sun says goodnight again
As the moon hold backs the clouds
With its perfect circle, it is full
As a hug, I stare at it with hope in my eyes.

POEM 64

Magic only shows itself
Only to the purest of souls
I met such a pure soul once
In the cafe where I sat for hours

Working on my projects
Staring at the screen
In front of me
With uncountable refills of my coffee

The aroma of baked goods, coffee
And vanilla, a mixture of several perfumes
Filled my mind
As I feel a sudden tap on shoulder.

That is when I found him
The purest souls
Followed by several angels
As he stared at me, with those dreamy eyes.

POEM 65

Those dreamy twilight black eyes
Stare at me, so deep
That it pierces my soul
A stare that can kill

Angels dressed in white gowns
Follow him behind
I keep staring at him
Like time had stopped

I could hear only
That deep husky voice of his
Which whispered in my ears
"We need to leave babe"

I looked at him with confusion
But all he did was smile at me
Suddenly he pulled me
And then everything was black.

POEM 66

There is one guy who protects me
And keeps me like a queen
He is perfection in the form of human
I often think how he came into my life

Then there is this other guy who acts like he doesn't care
But all the things he does
Like a hidden fairy
He is like a dream guy for most girls

Then comes another one who
Just uses you like his cars
Once he is bored and lonely
You will be kept like a queen.

My soul aches for all
But the only person I ever loved
Was you and no one can show
Me the world as you did.

The magical perfect world
For a princess to live in
You taught me how to live my dream
And I promise to never let you down.

POEM 67

I stare at the green in front of me
A giggle of strawberries
Sit amid the green
The dewdrops on the green grass

I step on the grass
As I feel the joy of the nature
I here laughter echoing in the air
The air filled with bubbles

The bubbles danced
In the breeze as if it were the slow dance of the prom.
They are like mirrors
Reflected with a swirl of rainbow rivers.

POEM 68

My sadness is not visible to everyone
I allow only a few
To know what life has shown me
I never found magic in life.

The 3 a.m. poetry flows through that sadness;
Sadness is in the songs that I listen to,
I put in the earphones as I am taken to the wonderland
Of powerful creatures, all colourful and magical-
A land full of colourful
Unicorns spreading their
Wings ready to fly
Reaching towards their destiny.

POEM 69

Bubble magic is in the air
Swans and unicorns
They are dancing in the sky
Rainbow splashed on their skin

I see the magic around me
Unicorns they say are nothing but myths
But the magical world that welcomed me
Has all the mythical joys in it.

POEM 70

All I do is sit and stare
At the blanket of stars
The constellations welcome me
With open arms

I look at the pretty
Colours splashed all around
I find magic in the air
We look for magic in others.

But have you ever looked at yourself
That beautiful smile
Those big doe eyes
The magic inside you shines like a gem.

POEM 71

I have shut myself out from this world
Slowly building walls around myself
All I did was create a concrete around me until
My back could feel the hardness of the wall

You taught me to never let down
These walls of mine
Cause when I did break these once for you
You turned my weakness into a game.

POEM 72

The memories of us running through
The screen of my mind made me feel the sudden ecstatic joy
Remembering your hands wrapped around my waist
I suddenly feel your phantom breath on my neck,
I dared to turn around, wanting to feel your touch
That my heart ached for.

POEM 73

Lonely days, rather weeks
Or even months,

I stopped talking to people
And going out made me feel nauseous,

Crowds made me feel claustrophobic
I pull myself under the blanket
Trying to feel the warmth as my body was frozen cold
I somehow scoot over to the edge of the bed

Curling up, trying to understand what went wrong.
I fail to recognise my own voice-
The voice in my head
Telling me to "MOVE ON"

The only voice that echoes in my mind is the one
That told "YOU ARE NOT ENOUGH!"

POEM 74

I saw the bird in all bright earthy hues
Looking at it carefully I realised
It had colours of the woodlands
I could hear it sing overhead

A little bird with beautiful woven feathers
Alighted upon the blossomed twig
It had a bonny bright soul
Which danced with the green lively leaves

It moved as if the world was its trampoline
And it takes its flight
Giving its colours to the sky
And I paused to see its silhouette against the dimming sky.

POEM 75

I don't know why i travelled to our favourite place
All alone, without any company
Maybe I still hoped that you would come back
I sat there ordering your favourite drink

I knew it was a strong drink
With the strong smell of alcohol
Seeping through my body
I feel the burn in my stomach

The alcohol slowly taking over my body
I had ordered your favourite
The food remained untouched
As I suddenly heard your laughter

I forced myself to turn around
I could feel the burn in my heart
As I saw you with her
She is beautiful and had a kind soul

I saw her legs tightly wrapped around you
And saw you looking at her full of love
I feel myself slowly fall on the counter
As a lone tear makes its way down my cheek.

POEM 76

You pointed out
To the sky,
From my balcony, my favourite place to
Let romance into our souls

As you slowly slide your hand into mine
You show me the Cassiopeia
near the end of spring break.

POEM 77

I will make myself forget every thing
And allow you to teach me constellations again
As we sit on our balcony,
Clinking our wine glasses,
As you whisper in my ear *"Cheers!"*
I could feel your warm breath on my ears
Sending shivers down my body.

POEM 78

I wait for you in the snow
Slowly humming out favourite song
Waiting for you to show up,
The sky was clear
And seemed to know my agony,
I stood there with a bouquet of roses and a bottle of
red wine
As I started to feel numb
The cold in the air did not bother me much,
My body and soul tired and exhausted of your
Empty promises, I dragged myself to my car
Cracking the window open
I stared at the sky
The constellations play in the winter sky
Inviting my soul to take a flight.

POEM 79

I sometimes feel like that there is rock placed on my chest-
A heavy object that can't be lifted
The weight of it pulling me down
I try to grab something from my bed but
I fail to find it,
The emptiness beside me scares me;
No wonder I always had the teddy bear
But once you came into my life
I had stuffed that somewhere safe in my heart.
But now that you are gone I will need him again to be my partner
In these lonely nights and keep my sheets warm.

POEM 80

I saw things you showed me and believed it
Knowing everything you said was just a lie
You told me I was overthinking and being paranoid
But now if I think about it
My biggest mistake was to believe
I was special.
When I saw you holding her and sitting
On the bench waiting for the first snow
And you forgot about me, the second I told it is over.
I saw you laugh and play our favourite song for her,
Taking her to our spot and riding our favourite rides
It was simply a cycle you followed,
My heart always aching for your touch,
I remind it how you broke us into a million pieces.

POEM 81

Memories of vivid hue come dancing in
As if the wind was their favourite tune,
I waltz with the music
My garden filled with your smell.
I dance like a bird wanting to fly
Looking up at the sky
I fell in love with the blue petal sky
That held summer dreams and winter love
Giving my dreams wings,
My heart fluttered towards ether.

ACKNOWLEDGEMENTS

My deepest thanks to my family; Shuvrangshu and Rupa Mazumder, I could never have asked for more supportive parents.

Thank you to my grandmother, uncle , aunt and my sweet little sister for always encouraging me.

Also I am thankful to my teachers who always encouraged and inspired me throughout my journey. Thank you the entire Clever Fox publishing team for helping me edit and publish this book.

I want to thank my friends, Anwayee, Meghna, Ujjayati and Rupanjana for helping me compile the poems into a book and for always motivating and inspiring me.

Last but not the least thank you to all my friends who have been there with me in some part of this journey, love you all.

www.ingramcontent.com/pod-product-compliance
Lightning Source LLC
LaVergne TN
LVHW041812060526
838201LV00046B/1233